P9-DXO-146

About This Book

Believe it or not, once upon a time, James and I were both kids.
Life was much easier in those days because there were rules most Americans
followed. Holding the door for someone. A nod and a hello.
Even just saying "please." Most kids did those things back then,
but now there is confusion in many places.
James and I believe we can bring that civility and compassion back into the
world. Let's start today with our children, by encouraging them to always say
that wonderful, magical word: *please*.

—Bill O'Reilly

BILL O'REILLY & JAMES PATTERSON

GIVE **PLEASE** A CHANCE

JIMMY PATTERSON BOOKS

LITTLE, BROWN AND COMPANY

NEW YORK BOSTON LONDON

Can I keep him?

Illustrated by Scott Magoon

Please?

Can I lick the bowl?

Illustrated by Tracy Dockray

Please?

Daddy, make the splinter go away.

Illustrated by Kate Babok

Please?

I've got a little problem. . . .

Illustrated by John Nez

Please?

Can I dress myself today?

Illustrated by Elizabet Vukovic

Please?

Can I have seconds?

Illustrated by Ziyue Chen

Please?

I need a friend.

Illustrated by Joe Sutphin

Please?

Zip me up!

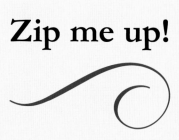

Illustrated by Frank Morrison

Please?

It's so hot out!

Illustrated by Ziyue Chen

Please?

Am I clean yet?

Illustrated by Daniel Roode

Please?

It's my favorite book. Ever!

Illustrated by Olga and Aleksey Ivanov

Please?

I am *too* big enough.

Illustrated by Alina Chau

Please?

Which part goes where?

Illustrated by Amy June Bates

Please?

Help! I'm stuck!

Illustrated by John Nez

Please?

Can we take them all?

Illustrated by Julie Robine

Please?

I really, really, really need a cookie!

Illustrated by Donald Wu

Please?

I can do that too!

Illustrated by Jennifer Zivoin

Please?

Trick and treat?

Illustrated by Begona Corbalan

Please?

Again! Again!

Illustrated by Ruth Galloway

Please?

Dear God, can you hear me?
I'm little.

Illustrated by Amy Bates

Please?

Swing me!

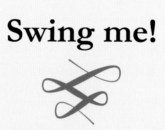

Illustrated by Tracy Dockray

Please?

I've been *extra* good this year.

Illustrated by Scott Magoon

peace ☮
and a few
more things:
teddy bear
pony
bike cat
computer
books
microphone
guitar+amp
concert tickets
parachute (red)
swimming pool
skateboard
trip to asia,
europe and to
okefenokee
swamp (to see
the alligators+
bears)
fabergé egg,
atv, rv, big
wheel, soccer
net, turtle,
saddle, singing
lessons, pottery
classes, bass guitar,
violin, drum set,
venus flytrap,
virtual reality goggles,
hockey mask, zipline,
zipline, yo-yo, atv
t golf clubs

air skis
baton
train
disco ball
tele
micro
scopes:
hairbrush!
skis, boots
back of it
jet engine on
scooter with
necklace
sharktooth
sketchbook
phone
yo-yo, jax

Please?

Can I get a hug?

Illustrated by Ruth Galloway

Please?

The characters and events in this book are fictitious. Any similarity to real persons, living or dead,
is coincidental and not intended by the authors.

Copyright © 2016 by William O'Reilly and James Patterson

Hachette Book Group supports the right to free expression and the value of copyright. The purpose of copyright is to encourage writers and artists to produce the creative
works that enrich our culture.
The scanning, uploading, and distribution of this book without permission is a theft of the authors' intellectual property. If you would like permission to use material from
the book (other than for review purposes), please contact permissions@hbgusa.com. Thank you for your support of the authors' rights.

JIMMY Patterson Books / Little, Brown and Company
Hachette Book Group
1290 Avenue of the Americas, New York, NY 10104
jimmypatterson.org

First Edition: November 2016

JIMMY Patterson Books is an imprint of Little, Brown and Company, a division of Hachette Book Group, Inc. The Little, Brown name and logo are
trademarks of Hachette Book Group, Inc. The JIMMY Patterson name and logo are trademarks of JBP Business, LLC.

The publisher is not responsible for websites (or their content) that are not owned by the publisher.

The Hachette Speakers Bureau provides a wide range of authors for speaking events. To find out more, go to hachettespeakersbureau.com or call (866) 376-6591.

Library of Congress Cataloging-in-Publication Data

Names: O'Reilly, Bill, author. | Patterson, James, author.
Title: Give please a chance / by Bill O'Reilly and James Patterson.
Description: First edition. | New York ; Boston : Little, Brown and Company,
2016. | "Jimmy Patterson Books." | Summary: "In this illustrated book
written by bestselling authors Bill O'Reilly and James Patterson, a
collection of artists each contribute a piece of art demonstrating why the
word 'please' makes all the difference in the world"—Provided by
publisher.
Identifiers: LCCN 2016014963| ISBN 978-0-316-27688-7 (hardcover) | ISBN
978-0-316-36174-3 (library edition ebook)
Subjects: | CYAC: Etiquette—Fiction.
Classification: LCC PZ7.1.O68 Gi 2016 | DDC [E]—dc23 LC record available at https://lccn.loc.gov/2016014963

10 9 8 7 6 5 4 3 2 1

Imago

Printed in China